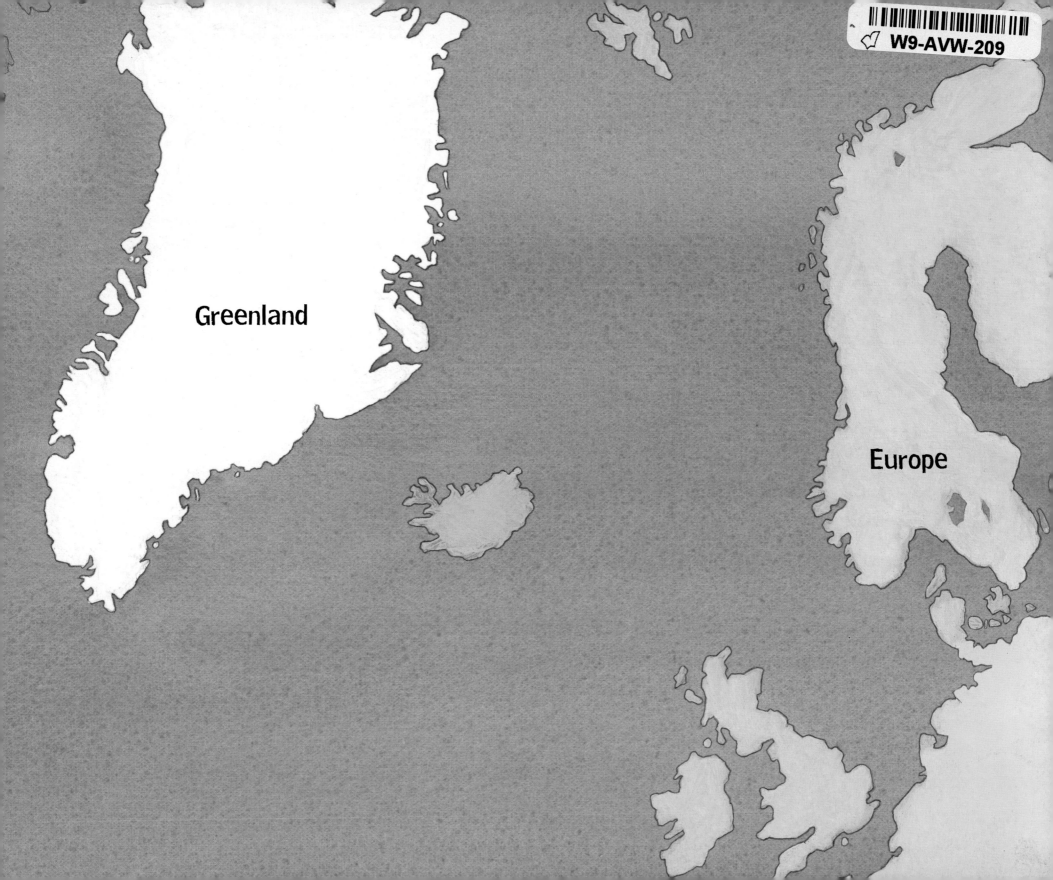

Greenland

Europe

Holtei / Vohwinkel, *Nanuk Will Fliegen*
© 2005 by Thienemann Verlag (Thienemann Verlag GmbH), Stuttgart / Wien

Published in 2008 by Eerdmans Books for Young Readers,
an imprint of Wm. B. Eerdmans Publishing Co.

Wm. B. Eerdmans Publishing Co.
2140 Oak Industrial Dr. NE, Grand Rapids, Michigan 49505
P.O. Box 163, Cambridge CB3 9PU U.K.

www.eerdmans.com/youngreaders

Manufactured in China

14 13 12 11 10 09 08   8 7 6 5 4 3 2 1

Library of Congress Cataloging-in-Publication Data

Holtei, Christa.
[Nanuk will fliegen. English]
Nanuk Flies Home / by Christa Holtei ; illustrated by Astrid Vohwinkel.
p. cm.
Summary: Captured by humans after trying to steal their food, a small, hungry polar bear cub
realizes his dream — to fly. End notes provide facts about polar bears and describe how, during
the month of October, several hundred polar bears gather in the small Canadian town of
Churchill, near the Hudson Bay, to wait for the sea to freeze over.

ISBN 978-0-8028-5342-4 (alk. paper)

[1. Polar bear — Fiction. 2. Bears — Fiction. 3. Flight — Fiction.] I. Vohwinkel, Astrid, ill. II. Title.
PZ7.H7419Nan 2008
[E]--dc22
                                    2007049342

Display type set in Hoosker
Text type set in Helvetica Neue

Nanuk Flies Home

Written by
Christa Holtei

Illustrated by
Astrid Vohwinkel

Eerdmans Books for Young Readers
Grand Rapids, Michigan   Cambridge, U.K.

Nanuk is grumpy. Very grumpy. Polar bear grumpy.
"It's boring here!" he grumbles, while trudging through
the snow with his mother Anaana.
Anaana nudges him with her big, black nose.
"Come on, just a few more steps," she says to cheer him up.

Nanuk runs up to some sea gulls. They rise up
into the cold winter air, squawking loudly.
"I wish I could fly, too," Nanuk grumbles.

Although he is such a small polar bear, Nanuk can do many things.

He can swim.

He can listen to the long stories Uppik the Snowy Owl likes to tell.

He can roll around in the snow.

He can dig deep holes in the snow.

And he can wander about on the snow and ice with his mother Anaana for hours and hours. When he is tired, he simply crawls onto her warm, furry back and sleeps a little.

The only thing Nanuk cannot do is fly. He would get home much faster if he could.

Nanuk's home is the wide, snowy plain up in the North with holes in the ice where he can fish. Fish — yummy! Nanuk can feel his tummy getting grumpy. Even grumpier than he is. Nanuk is as hungry as the biggest polar bear.

"Anaana, I'm hungry!" he wails.

"I'm hungry, too!" Anaana says. "Let's go to the humans' settlement. We can always find something to eat there."

Nanuk closes his eyes and dreams of home — a huge, snow-white plain.

Anaana ambles towards a hill. It smells good.
Nanuk follows her curiously, sniffing around a little.

"This doesn't taste good," he says after nibbling
some garbage.

"That's because you can't eat that," laughs Anaana,
shaking her head.

Nanuk tugs at an old leather bag until he has torn it
to pieces. Then he sits down in the snow with a thump.
   "It's boring here, very boring."
   "Follow me," says Anaana.

The settlement is totally different from how Nanuk imagined it to be. There are a lot of street signs everywhere. And the snow on the houses and frozen roads doesn't look very white.

Strange machines on wheels or runners make a horrible noise as they roar away. They turn every last bit of white snow into gray slush. Is there really something to eat in this place? Nanuk is very disappointed. "It's boring here," he mutters, but only very quietly so Anaana cannot hear him.

Nanuk has never seen humans before. There are small ones and big ones, just like Nanuk and Anaana. Some of them scream and run away.

Anaana pushes open a door with her nose. Nanuk cannot believe his eyes. There are fruits and fish and vegetables. He does not know where to start.

A human comes to the door, but Nanuk does not see him.

Nanuk does not know what has happened, but he wakes up in a dark cage. Anaana is lying beside him, sleeping.

"Help!" Nanuk squeaks anxiously. "Anaana?"

"What is the matter, little one?" It is the deep voice of another polar bear in the next cage.

"Where are we?" Nanuk asks, unsure of himself. "And why doesn't Anaana say anything?"

"This is the Polar Bear Jail," the bear answers. "And your Anaana is fine. She'll wake up soon. The same thing has happened to me now for the second time. How careless of me to let them catch me stealing food!"

"But why is Anaana asleep?" Nanuk asks.

"The humans gave you and Anaana a tranquilizer, a shot of medicine to put you to sleep. You just woke up earlier than she did," the polar bear explains.

"But why?"

"They are afraid of us. We're not exactly nice when we're hungry. *Dangerous* is more like it. That's why they catch us and put us here in the Polar Bear Jail. Sometime soon we'll fly out to the icy plain where we belong."

Nanuk is very excited. "We'll fly?"
Only sea gulls and snowy owls can fly;
he is sure about that.

"You'll fly with a machine," the polar bear tells him. "And then you'll be back on the icy plain with its many fishing holes."
Nanuk can hardly wait. He gets fidgety and nudges Anaana.

"Anaana, we'll be flying home soon!" he cries excitedly. Anaana blinks one eye.

"Nonsense!" she mumbles. "Polar bears can't fly." And then she falls fast asleep again.

Very soon Nanuk hears the big roar of a machine.
The gate opens and a human who looks friendly calls out,
"The female with the cub first!"
Nanuk allows himself to be carried to the noisy machine
and fastened to the seat with a belt.

Then he goes up in the sky! Nanuk
feels his tummy tingling as the ground
drifts farther and farther away. Flying is
so exciting! He looks out of the window
and down at the tiny houses. There is
Anaana, too. She is in a big cargo net,
floating under the machine. She is still
sleeping. She will miss everything!

Now the snow becomes whiter and whiter. Some places glimmer gray as glass where the ocean is frozen. The white dots down there are polar bears. Nanuk giggles. They have to walk, but he can fly! Now he can see the wide, snowy plain with its many fishing holes, and sea gulls, and Uppik the Snowy Owl with her long stories.

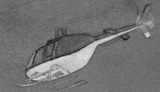

This is Nanuk's home. He is very glad to be back.
The flying machine slowly comes down to the ice.
Anaana gently lands on the ground in her cargo net.
Soon Nanuk is sitting beside her.

He knows that Anaana is going to wake up any minute. She is already blinking. Then he will tell her the most exciting story she has ever heard. Not even Uppik the Snowy Owl knows such a story. It is the story of Nanuk and how he flew.

Soon they will go fishing and roll in the snow and romp around. It is much better here than in the humans' settlement because here, on the icy, snowy plain,

Nanuk is at home.

Polar Bear Capital of the World — Churchill, Manitoba, Canada

Every year in mid-October, hundreds of polar bears gather in the small town of Churchill on the west coast of Hudson Bay in Manitoba, Canada. They wait there for the sea to freeze over. It is only on the pack ice that they can find enough food to eat.

The polar bears are hungry! During the summer they live off only leaves, fruit, and grass, which they find on the mainland, and off their own fat. That is not enough for a grown polar bear.

Hungry polar bears are dangerous. They search for food everywhere—in garbage dumps, in shops, and in private kitchens. Sometimes they even attack humans. That is why Churchill has a Polar Bear Alert Program with an emergency number that can be reached 24 hours a day, and a polar bear jail.

Canadian wildlife officials shoot the bears with tranquilizer guns and take them to the Polar Bear Compound, or Polar Bear Jail, outside Churchill. The bears are marked so that they can be recognized later. They are not given anything to eat because polar bears are smart—they would definitely come back next year looking for food!

In the Polar Bear Jail they sleep and gather strength. When the sea is frozen, a helicopter—the Polar Bear Taxi—flies them north in cargo nets. The polar bear cubs are also drugged during the flight, because if not, they would snap and bite. They are fastened to a seat inside the helicopter. It would be too cold for them in the cargo net, but adult bears do not mind the freezing air. When they wake up again, they are finally where they belong: on the endless plain of ice in the North.